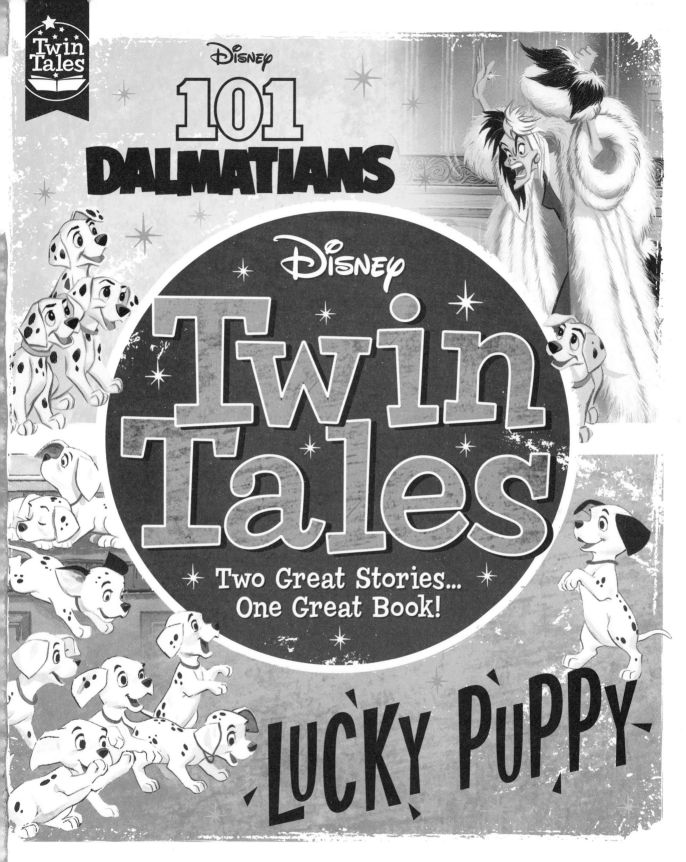

Disney

101 DALMATIANS

Disney Twin Tales

Two Great Stories...
One Great Book!

LUCKY PUPPY

AUTUMN
PUBLISHING

AUTUMN
PUBLISHING

Published in 2021
First published in the UK by Autumn Publishing
An imprint of Igloo Books Ltd
Cottage Farm, NN6 0BJ, UK
Owned by Bonnier Books
Sveavägen 56, Stockholm, Sweden
www.igloobooks.com

© 2021 Disney Enterprises, Inc.
Based on the book *The Hundred and One Dalmatians*
by Dodie Smith, published by The Viking Press.

1221 001
2 4 6 8 10 9 7 5 3 1
ISBN 978-1-80022-317-2

Printed and manufactured in China

This book belongs to:

....

101 Dalmatians

It was a sad day for Roger and Anita. Their two Dalmatians had recently had fifteen perfect puppies. But tragedy struck soon after – the puppies had been stolen! Despite the story being front-page news, no one knew where the puppies were.

The two Dalmatian parents, Pongo and Perdita, were very sad, too. But neither of them were ready to give up. Pongo's owner, Roger, suspected Cruella De Vil – an old school friend of Anita's – had stolen the puppies.

There was nothing Roger could do to prove it, however, so the two dogs decided it was up to them to find their puppies. It was time for the Twilight Bark!

The Twilight Bark was a system of long and short barks used by dogs to pass along news.

On Pongo and Perdita's walk that very evening, the pair barked long and loud. They wanted all the dogs in London to be on the lookout for their puppies.

Soon, they heard a reply. It was from a Great Dane, who relayed the message about the missing puppies to every other dog within range.

That night, the Twilight Bark reached as
far as a quiet farm, where a sheepdog, known
as Colonel, lifted a shaggy ear to listen. He
explained to Sergeant Tibbs – his cat friend –
that the message was about fifteen Dalmatian
puppies who had been stolen.

"Two nights past, I heard puppy barking,"
said Tibbs, pointing to the De Vil manor.

Colonel and Sergeant Tibbs decided to
investigate.

The stolen puppies were at Cruella's manor! And not just them – there were eighty-four more.

Colonel went back to the farm and used the Twilight Bark to let Pongo and Perdita know they had found their puppies. The pair of them set off across the snowy countryside at once.

Meanwhile, Tibbs kept an eye on the puppies.

The next day, Cruella arrived. She was telling her two henchmen, Horace and Jasper, her evil plan.

"You couldn't get half a dozen coats out of the whole caboodle," complained one of the henchmen.

"Then we'll settle for half a dozen," said Cruella, before roaring off again in her car.

Tibbs couldn't believe his furry ears. They were going to turn the puppies into coats! He knew he had to help them escape before it was too late!

"Hey, kids," said Tibbs to the pups. "You'd better get out of here if you want to save your skins."

He shoved one of the puppies towards a hole in the wall. One by one, the puppies followed Tibbs away from the two henchmen.

Suddenly, Horace and Jasper realised that the puppies were escaping. Tibbs and the puppies scooted through the dark halls of the manor, desperately trying to escape the clutches of the two baddies.

Meanwhile, Colonel had met up with Perdita and Pongo and had led them to the manor house. The two Dalmatians rushed through the open gates of the manor, hoping that they weren't too late to save their puppies.

Horace and Jasper had Tibbs and the puppies cornered. But suddenly, Pongo and Perdita came bursting into the manor and immediately attacked the thugs.

The angry Dalmatian parents fought off the surprised men as all the puppies, with the help of Tibbs, scampered to safety.

Leaving Horace and Jasper in a heap on the floor, Perdita and Pongo dashed after the puppies.

"Everybody here?" asked Pongo. "All fifteen?"

"Twice that many, Dad," replied one of the puppies. "Now there's ninety-nine of us."

The puppies explained what Cruella wanted them for.

Pongo and Perdita were shocked and decided to take all the puppies back to London with them so they'd be safe.

The group hurried back across the countryside, towards London and home. Pongo and Perdita led the way, their fifteen puppies and all the others right behind them.

Horace and Jasper weren't far behind, though, and the group had to hide to avoid being spotted.

Eventually, the group of tired Dalmatians arrived at a small town. They met a friendly black Labrador who arranged for them to ride to London in a van that was parked nearby.

Suddenly, Cruella's big car pulled up outside. Somehow, she had followed their tracks.

Two of the pups began messing around in some soot and became completely covered in black. This gave Pongo an idea. He decided they should all roll in the soot – that way, they would look just like black Labradors.

When everyone was ready, the dogs marched outside.
One after another, the soot-covered puppies were lifted into
the van. Before Pongo had a chance to pick up the last one,
a clump of snow fell from the shed onto the puppy.

Pongo quickly snatched up the pup, but the snow washed
away the soot. Cruella, who was searching the town for the
Dalmatians, could see the white fur and black spots she longed
for so much.

The van began to pull away, but Pongo and the final pup weren't inside! Pongo, with the pup in his mouth, rushed to catch up. They managed to jump inside just in time.

But Cruella was hot on their heels. The van was going fast, but Cruella was going faster. She was soon alongside the van, trying to ram it off the road – much to the surprise of the driver, who had no idea why Cruella was behaving that way.

Behind them, a van driven by Horace and Jasper was following. They decided to take another path to cut off the other van's route.

Pongo and Perdita watched on as their van bounced and bumped along the snowy road. They hoped it wouldn't crash, and that they, and the puppies, would escape the evil Cruella De Vil.

Luckily, their hopes were realised as the van driven by Horace and Jasper missed their van completely, and drove into the side of Cruella's car! Both vehicles slid into a ditch and the Dalmatians escaped.

The last they saw of Cruella, she was having a nasty temper tantrum.

When the van reached London, Pongo, Perdita and all the puppies found their way back to Roger and Anita's house. They had made it home safe and sound.

Roger was overjoyed to see Pongo again, and gave him a big hug, as well as giving hugs to Perdita and all the pups, too.

Anita began counting up all the dogs in their house.

"A hundred and one!" she declared. "What will we do with them?"

"We'll keep them!" cried Roger, happily.

"In this little house?" asked Anita.

"We'll buy a big place in the country," replied Roger.

And they did exactly that. Pongo, Perdita and all the spotted
puppies lived happily ever after.

Lucky Puppy

Lucky Puppy lived with his father, Pongo, his mother, Perdita, and all his brothers and sisters. The people who belonged to them were Roger and Anita and Nanny Cook. That's Nanny Cook in the doorway.

Here are Penny and Lenny, and Salter and Pepper! And Jolly and Rolly, and Patch and Latch.

Here are Spot and Dot, and Blob and Blot, and Billy and
Wally, and— where's Lucky?

Here is Lucky in front of the television. He is
watching his favourite show, *Thunderbolt*.

Whenever Penny and Lenny wanted to dig holes…

… or Salter and Pepper wanted to chew bones…

… or Patch and Latch
wanted to chase tails…

… or Jolly and Rolly wanted to jump
at Nanny Cook's apron strings…

… or Spot and Dot wanted to play hide-and-seek…

… or Blob and Blot wanted to growl at the mirror…

… or Billy and Wally wanted to take a nap, Lucky never wanted to. He just wanted to sit in front of the television watching *Thunderbolt*.

Or he practised television tricks. "I'm going to be a television star myself," said Lucky.

Well, all the other puppies learnt puppy tricks.
Soon they could sit up and roll over.

They could dance
and shake hands.

They could jump for a treat
and walk politely at heel.

But not Lucky. He was too busy
dreaming of being a television star.

One day he decided he was ready to be in a
television show. So he slipped out of the house
and ran down the street.

He ran round a corner. And then stopped. He was
lost. Lucky did not know his way to the television
place. And he did not know his way home.

Poor Lucky. He walked and walked and walked. He tried to show people his television tricks, but they did not understand. "He doesn't seem to know any puppy tricks," was all the people said.

Finally, a policeman came along. He looked
at Lucky's collar and took him home.

There were Penny and Lenny, and Salter and Pepper, and Jolly and Rolly, and Patch and Latch.

Along with Spot and Dot, Blob and Blot, and Billy and Wally. They were all doing puppy tricks for treats. But not Lucky.

Lucky was all tired out. He crept into his
basket and went straight to sleep.

He even slept through the *Thunderbolt*
show, which the other puppies watched.

But the next morning, Lucky was up first.
"Plenty of time for television later," he said.
"Now I am going to learn puppy tricks."
    And he did.